Dear Parent:
Your child's love of reading starts here!

Every child learns to read in a different way and at his or her own speed. Some go back and forth between reading levels and read favorite books again and again. Others read through each level in order. You can help your young reader improve and become more confident by encouraging his or her own interests and abilities. From books your child reads with you to the first books he or she reads alone, there are I Can Read Books for every stage of reading:

SHARED READING
Basic language, word repetition, and whimsical illustrations, ideal for sharing with your emergent reader

BEGINNING READING
Short sentences, familiar words, and simple concepts for children eager to read on their own

READING WITH HELP
Engaging stories, longer sentences, and language play for developing readers

READING ALONE
Complex plots, challenging vocabulary, and high-interest topics for the independent reader

ADVANCED READING
Short paragraphs, chapters, and exciting themes for the perfect bridge to chapter books

I Can Read Books have introduced children to the joy of reading since 1957. Featuring award-winning authors and illustrators and a fabulous cast of beloved characters, I Can Read Books set the standard for beginning readers.

A lifetime of discovery begins with the magical words **"I Can Read!"**

Visit www.icanread.com for information
on enriching your child's reading experience.

For Mimi—a friend
forever
—R.P.G.

For A.B.: my long-sleeve
plaid flannel friend
—T.E.

HarperCollins®, ☷®, and I Can Read Book® are trademarks of HarperCollins Publishers.

Library of Congress Cataloging-in-Publication Data
O'Connor, Jane.
  Pajama Day / by Jane O'Connor ; cover illustration by Robin Preiss Glasser ; interior pencils by Ted Enik ; color by Carolyn Bracken. — 1st ed.
    p. cm. — (Fancy Nancy) (I can read! Level 1)
  Summary: Nancy, who likes to use fancy words, is excited to wear her elegant nightgown for Pajama Day at school, until her best friend, Bree, and Clara impress everyone by wearing matching pink polka-dot pajamas.
  ISBN 978-0-06-170370-6 (pbk.) — ISBN 978-0-06-170371-3 (trade bdg.)
  [1. Pajamas—Fiction. 2. Friendship—Fiction. 3. Schools—Fiction. 4. Vocabulary—Fiction.] I. Enik, Ted, ill. II. Title.
PZ7.O222Paj 2009   2008027472
[E]—dc22   CIP
                                                                                                                    AC

10 11 12 13   LP/WOR   10 9 8 7 6 5 4   ❖   First Edition

I Can Read! — BEGINNING READING 1

Fancy NANCY Pajama Day

by Jane O'Connor

cover illustration by Robin Preiss Glasser

interior pencils by Ted Enik

color by Carolyn Bracken

HarperCollinsPublishers

"Class, don't forget!"
Ms. Glass says.
"Tomorrow is . . ."
"Pajama Day!" we shout in unison.
(That's a fancy word
for all together.)

I plan to wear my new nightgown.

I must say, it is very elegant!

(Elegant is a fancy word

for fancy.)

Then the phone rings.

It is Bree.

She says, "I am going to wear
my pajamas with pink hearts
and polka dots.

Do you want to wear yours?

We can be twins!"

"Ooh!" I say.

"Being twins would be fun."

Then I look at my elegant nightgown.

What a dilemma!

(That's a fancy word for problem.)

9

Finally I make up my mind.

I tell Bree I am going to wear

my brand-new nightgown.

Bree understands.

She is my best friend.

She knows how much

I love being fancy.

The next morning at school,
we can't stop laughing.
Everyone's in pajamas,
even the principal.
He is carrying a teddy bear.

Ms. Glass has on a long nightshirt
and fuzzy slippers.
I am the only one
in a fancy nightgown.
That makes me unique!
(You say it like this: you-NEEK.)

"Nancy, look!" says Bree.

"Clara has on the same

pajamas as me."

Bree and Clara giggle.

"We're twins!" says Clara.

"And we didn't even plan it."

At story hour, Ms. Glass

has us spread out our blankets.

She reads a bedtime story.

Clara and Bree lie
next to each other.
"We're twins,"
Clara keeps saying.

At recess

Clara takes Bree's hand.

They run to the monkey bars.

"Come on, Nancy," Bree calls.

18

But it is hard to climb in
a long nightgown.
And I can't hang upside down.
Everyone would see
my underpants!

At lunch

I sit with Bree and Clara.

They both have grape rolls

in their lunch boxes.

"Isn't that funny, Nancy?"

asks Clara.

"We even have the same dessert."

I do not reply.

(That's a fancy word for answer.)

Pajama Day is not turning out

to be much fun.

I wanted to be fancy and unique.

Instead I feel excluded.

(That's fancy for left out.)

The afternoon is no better.

Clara and Bree are partners

in folk dancing.

Robert steps on my hem.

Some of the lace trim

on my nightgown rips.

At last the bell rings.

I am glad Pajama Day is over.

"Do you want to come
play at my house?"
I ask Bree.

But Bree can't come.

She's going to Clara's house!

I know it's immature.

(That's fancy for babyish.)

But I almost start to cry.

Then, as we are leaving,

Bree and Clara rush over.

"Nancy, can you come play too?"

Clara asks.

"Yes!" I say.

"I just have to go home first
to change."

Now we are triplets!

Fancy Nancy's Fancy Words

These are the fancy words in this book:

Dilemma—a problem

Elegant—fancy

Excluded—left out

Immature—babyish

Reply—answer

Unique—one of a kind (you say it like this: you-NEEK)

Unison—all together